W9-BTF-330

ILLUMINATION PRESENTS

DESPICABLE
ME 3 ™

Little, Brown and Company
Hachette Book Group
1290 Avenue of the Americas, New York, NY 10104
Visit us at lb-kids.com
www.despicable.me

First Edition: May 2017

Little, Brown and Company is a division of Hachette Book Group, Inc. The Little, Brown name and logo are trademarks of Hachette Book Group, Inc.

The publisher is not responsible for websites (or their content) that are not owned by the publisher.

Library of Congress Control Number 2017934040

ISBNs: 978-0-316-50754-7 (pbk.), 978-0-316-50756-1 (hardcover), 978-0-316-50752-3 (ebook)

Printed in the United States of America

LSC-C

10 9 8 7 6 5 4 3 2 1

ILLUMINATION PRESENTS

DESPICABLE ME 3 ™

The Junior Novel

Adapted by Sadie Chesterfield

Based on the Motion Picture Screenplay
written by Cinco Paul and Ken Daurio

Little, Brown and Company
New York · Boston

CHAPTER 1

/////////////////////

Balthazar Bratt peered through his binoculars at the tanker ship in the distance. Armed guards paced the length of the deck, scanning the horizon. They didn't notice his boat floating in the background. Bratt turned to Clive, his robot sidekick, and thought back to the path that'd brought him there.

Bratt had come so far since 1985, back when he was the child star of the number-one show on television, *Evil Bratt*. He'd played a child prodigy and criminal mastermind bent on world domination. He became known for two things: blowing bubbles with his pink bubble gum and uttering his famous catchphrase. "I've been a bad boy!" he'd sneer after every hideous misdeed.

Bratt became the biggest child actor of the 1980s, striking a chord with audiences all over the world. Soon his face was on lunch boxes and posters. There were *Evil Bratt* action figures and video games. For years it seemed as if no mug or pair of pajamas could escape his wicked grin.

But Bratt's career came to an end in season three, when he experienced an unexpected growth spurt. Now taller, and perhaps a little awkward-looking, Bratt battled his enemies, but was no longer a cute little kid. Every time he tried to utter his famous catchphrase, his voice cracked. Soon the show was canceled.

Bratt shuddered as he thought back to those dark days. Instead of falling into the Hollywood abyss, he'd become obsessed with the character he played on television. Soon he was just as infamous and evil as Evil Bratt himself.

"You know what, Clive?" he said between chews of his gum. "Playing a villain on TV was fun—but being one in real life is even better. Heist music!"

Clive slipped a tape into the boat's tape deck. A sweet, soulful melody filled the air.

"What? Clive!" Balthazar yelled. "What are you doing? How is that heist music?"

"Sorry, my bad." Clive ejected the tape and flipped it to the "Heist Music" side before popping it back in. Suddenly Michael Jackson's "Bad" was blasting from the speakers. Bratt pulled on his scuba gear and dove off the side of the boat.

He swam underneath the waves, popping up near the side of the massive ship. He moonwalked across the water and climbed up the side to the deck. When he was just a few feet from the top, he blew a bubble with his gum and tossed it onto the ship. Within seconds, a guard stepped on it.

"Ewww!" the guard yelled. "Wha-whoa! Gah!"

The bubble gum was Bratt's secret weapon. As the guard lifted his foot, the gum grew to twice its original size; then it expanded even more, covering the deck of the ship. It was like the Blob, only bigger and faster and pinker. Within just a few seconds, it had completely engulfed the guards and was oozing down the sides of the ship.

Bratt hopped onto the deck, moving

easily around the gum as the last of the guards were swallowed into the sticky pink mass. Bratt dropped down a manhole and went deeper into the ship, searching for his prize.

CHAPTER 2

Lucy and Gru sped through the water in their miniature submarines. Behind them in a miniature submarine, two of Gru's Minions, Tony and Steve, cut through a patch of seaweed. They were doing surveillance for the Anti-Villain League, also known as the AVL. Now that Gru had changed his life for the better, he made his living capturing villains across the globe.

The radio crackled. They heard their boss from AVL, Silas Ramsbottom, speaking to someone. "Balthazar Bratt! Blast it! The

Dupont Diamond is on that ship!" he said. "I want every agent in the area on the scene immediately."

Lucy scanned the radar, realizing he was talking about a tanker ship nearby. They'd been patrolling the ocean in case something like this happened. Gru had gone up against Balthazar Bratt before, and he was ready to do it again.

"We're already here!" Lucy said into her earpiece. "Agents Grucy are closing in fast."

"Yes—wait, wha? What did you call us?" her husband, Gru, asked.

"Grucy. You know, Gru and Lucy mushed together. Try it," Lucy urged.

"Haha. I like it, but not a lot," Gru said. "I don't like it."

They rushed across the ocean, finally coming up when they were just yards from the massive ship. It was covered in Bratt's signature gooey pink gum. It bubbled and oozed in places and was filled with a toxic gas that resembled helium, which caused the ship to float. The ship rose up out of the water, higher and higher in the air. Lucy and Gru could see Balthazar Bratt climbing the staircase on deck, the Dupont Diamond in his hands.

"He's getting away!!" Gru cried.

"That's what he thinks," Lucy said. Their mini-subs transformed into high-tech rocket-powered hydra-cycles. Tony and Steve's mini-submarine turned into a waterwheel bicycle.

"*Wahooo!*" Tony and Steve screamed. "Go, go, go!"

Lucy had her foot pressed down on the gas, pushing the engine as far as it would go. They were moving as fast as they could, but the giant ship was already out of the water. It floated higher with each passing second.

"Get ready!" she yelled as they approached.

Gru looked at his wife. "Get ready for *whaaa—*"

Lucy hit a button on the dash, blasting the water beneath their hydra-cycles. Gru, Tony, and Steve were ejected and were sent flying through the air toward the ship. Gru landed on the deck, but the Minions were so light they flew a hundred yards farther, crashing down on a tourist beach.

Gru had barely gotten up when he heard a familiar voice.

"Hello, Gru," Balthazar sneered. "How's your transition coming? You know, from world's worst villain to world's worst agent?"

"Oh, that's hilarious!" Gru said, striking back. "You should be on TV! Oh, that's right, you were—but then you got canceled."

Balthazar pointed his huge gun at Gru, but Gru punched him before he could shoot. Then Gru pulled out an even bigger gun. Balthazar knocked that out of his hand and drew an even bigger gun.

Gru pushed it away from him. Then he reached into his pocket, pulling out . . . a green plastic water gun. Not quite what he was expecting.

"Oh! Girls . . . ," he said, realizing Agnes or Edith must've put it in there.

Gru squirted Bratt, but then he threw the gun at Bratt's face. Gru went to punch Bratt, but Bratt managed to dodge his blows.

"Dance fight!" Bratt yelled.

The two danced and fought, and danced and fought some more. Then Gru saw his chance. He punched Bratt right in his nose, knocking him out cold. He laughed as he picked up the Dupont Diamond.

"Alpha team," he said into his headset. "The diamond is secure. Come and pick up the package."

Within minutes, Gru spotted helicopters in the distance, approaching the floating ship. The AVL team had gotten him support faster than he'd hoped. He was so happy that it took him a second to notice Bratt standing behind him. His Keytar was aimed at Gru's chest. The weapon was a cross between a guitar and a keyboard, and it created sounds so powerful they could bring a man to his knees.

"Did you actually think I was unconscious?" Bratt asked. "It's called acting, hoser! And clearly I've still got it!"

He laughed as he played his Keytar, which sent out a sonic blast at Gru. It was so intense Gru fell off the ship, and his clothes ripped off his body piece by piece. First his shirt . . .

then his pants. His shoes . . . his socks. Even his underwear.

Let's just say it was a teensy bit embarrassing.

He kept falling, naked as a baby, over the side of the ship. He bounced off a bubble-gum bubble on the way down. The gum stuck to his butt, which kept him from falling another hundred yards to his death. Gru hung from the ship by one gooey glob of gum.

Balthazar Bratt stared down at Gru. He laughed hysterically. "I've been a *baaaaaaaad* boy!" he yelled.

Just then the AVL helicopters descended on the ship deck. Agents surrounded Bratt. "Freeze! Don't move!" one yelled.

But Bratt just leapt off the deck of the ship. He activated his wingsuit, flying out over the ocean. "This isn't over, Gru!" he called out behind him. "You hear me? This is not over!"

"Well, I still have the diamond!" Gru yelled. He held it tight as the ship floated through the city. He was hanging, still secured by the sticky piece of gum. The ship floated on, passing a skyscraper. Inside it a dozen office workers were celebrating someone's birthday. They pointed and laughed at Gru as he floated past their window.

"Happy birthday, dear *Daaaaaan*," Gru sang quietly to himself as he tried to pretend he wasn't naked. "Happy birthday to you."

CHAPTER 3

Gru turned the car in to the parking lot of the Sunset Retirement Home. The wheels screeched as he slammed his foot on the brake.

"And it's not just that Bratt got away!" he said. "It's that he's so smug about it!"

Lucy got out of the car and walked inside, Gru following behind her. His face was still pink from his rant. She said hello to the receptionist, and they passed the common room. Two mannequins in gray wigs sat beside each other on the couch.

"And it was just so humiliating," Gru went on. "Dangling there in the bubble-gum Speedo."

He picked up the old woman mannequin and moved her to the coatrack. Lucy did the same with the old man mannequin. Then they both sat down on the couch. Gru scanned his palm print on the arm of the couch as he continued on.

"And I didn't have time to go to the gym this week! And I had a big breakfast! I was feeling a little bloated!"

The sofa propelled them up to the top floors of the building. They rode it through the streets and into the air, soaring toward the AVL blimp.

"You know what? He's not even worth talking about. I don't even want to waste another breath about the guy." He sighed, but it wasn't more than two seconds before he remembered something else. "And another thing!"

As they got to the blimp lobby, Lucy and Gru walked past another receptionist.

"Next time I see Bratt, I will moonwalk all over his stupid face!" Gru said.

Inside the auditorium, Silas Ramsbottom was already onstage. He was a huge man with a neck that spilled over his collar. The audience was filled with AVL agents. "It is with great sadness that I inform you that as of today I am being replaced as the head of the AVL."

A few agents in the crowd gasped. One started sobbing.

"Anyway," Silas said, "your new leader is coming directly from head office, effective immediately. She is the very gifted, very ambitious Miss Valerie Da Vinci."

A young, tough-looking woman stepped

onto the stage. She looked very put together and professional. Silas smiled at her and then continued, "As I look out over all of your faces, I am flooded with so many memories. I—"

"Blah blah blah," Valerie interrupted. "We understand. You're old, you're fat, you're done."

He lowered down into a hatch in the floor. Valerie pushed him in the rest of the way, slamming the door behind him.

"First order of business," she said, scanning the crowd. "Which one of you losers is Agent Gru?"

Gru stiffened. "Uh . . . that would be me. Although I don't know if I'd say 'loser' per se, kind of a—"

Before he could finish, his phone rang. It was his adopted daughters. He fumbled with the phone, trying to switch the ringer to silent, but he couldn't figure out how.

"Hey!" Valerie yelled. She stepped down from the stage, approaching him. "How could you let Balthazar Bratt, the AVL's most-wanted villain, just get away? That is the opposite of what we do here!"

Gru took a step back.

"Okay, okay, yes, maybe he got away," he said. "Again—but he didn't get the diamond! And I am this close to bringing him in. *This close!*"

Valerie looked him up and down. "Uh-huh. Okay. You're off the case."

Gru glanced sideways at Lucy, who seemed stunned.

"What?" he asked. "You can't do that! Look at my record: I've caught El Macho."

"Doppelgänger," Lucy added.

"Doppelgänger," Gru repeated.

"Argue-tron . . ."

"Argue-tron!" Gru said. "Boy, that guy

was tough. He kept complaining, like 'No, you didn't catch me.' "

"Huh. Interesting." Valerie brought her finger to her chin, as if she were deep in thought. "You know what? I've changed my mind. You're not off the case."

"I'm not?" Gru smiled.

"No. You're fired!" she yelled.

"Whaaaaaaat?" Gru said, barely able to get the word out.

Lucy couldn't take it anymore. Who did this Da Vinci character think she was, talking to Gru like that? Acting like he was a big nobody?

"Gru is a great agent!" Lucy said, pointing a finger in Valerie's face. "You know what? If you fire him, you're going to have to fire me, sister sister. And do you really want to do that? Do ya?"

Valerie didn't bother answering. Instead

she pointed to two agents who grabbed Gru and Lucy by their arms and led them to the door of the blimp. The receptionist handed them each a box and then—*whomp!*—they were given a swift kick out.

"Well, I guess she did!" Lucy yelled as they fell ten stories through the sky, plummeting toward earth.

Their parachutes opened as they cascaded toward the ground. It didn't feel real. Was Gru's life at AVL really ending so soon after it had begun?

CHAPTER 4

■●▲●●▲●▲●●▲■

Lucy and Gru stood on the front stoop of the house, just staring at each other. They didn't want to go in. On the other side of that door was real life—Agnes, Edith, and Margo. They were so smart. It was only a matter of time before they realized something was up.

"We're going to have to tell the girls," Lucy said.

Gru let out a deep sigh. He turned to the door, noticing that it was open the tiniest bit.

What could this mean? Could an intruder have entered their home? Gru and Lucy were immediately suspicious. Gru made some birdcalls. Lucy added a few spy signals. No one responded.

Walking carefully inside, Gru waited for Agnes, Edith, and Margo to run to greet them . . . but nothing happened. Inside, the living room was completely dark. They didn't hear a sound. Something was off. "Hello?" Gru said finally, peering around the room.

One of the girls ran up behind them, throwing a bag over Gru's head. Another blindfolded Lucy and pushed both Lucy and Gru into rolling chairs. Within seconds, they were being rushed through the house and out the back door, into the yard.

The girls removed Lucy's blindfold and the bag from Gru's head, revealing a dinner with Hawaiian-themed lights and decorations. The dinner was perched high on the deck of the tree house. Lights crisscrossed the yard as Edith recorded their reactions with her camera.

"Aloha!" the girls cried.

"This is unexpected," Gru said.

"Well, you never got to go on a honeymoon, so . . . ," Margo, their oldest daughter, said.

"We made you dinner!" Edith cried. She was wearing the pink striped hat she never took off.

Agnes, the tiniest of their girls, ran around in circles. She jumped up and down, her black ponytail bouncing. She was so full of enthusiasm, and almost everything she did made Gru smile.

"It's a luau!" she said. "We got pineapples and coconuts and lukuleles!"

Two Minions, Dave and Jerry, started a song on their ukuleles. They were both in

Hawaiian gear: grass skirts and coconut bras. "Ya malatika tika, hee ha!" they sang. "Oww oww oww ah ah ah!"

Margo and Edith led Lucy up into the tree house to a table set for two. Gru pulled himself up via a pulley system. Once they were settled, Agnes placed two bowls in front of them containing some sort of soup.

"Looks too good to even eat!" Gru said, staring at the bowl in front of him.

Agnes frowned. "But I made it for you. . . ."

Gru shoved a giant spoonful in his mouth, trying to keep the smile on his face. *"Mmmmmm . . . ,"* he said, slapping the table. "Good soup! I love the combination of gummy bears and meat!"

"I'm gonna hold it in my mouth," Lucy said, "because it's so good I don't want to swallow it."

"How was work?" Margo asked.

Gru and Lucy exchanged a worried look. Then Gru cleared his throat.

"Well, actually, today Lucy and I were invited . . . to not work at the AVL anymore."

The Minions stopped playing their song. The whole yard was quiet.

"You got *fired*?" Margo asked, holding her hands to her cheeks.

"Oh no! No, no, no." Gru laughed then got suddenly serious. "Yes."

"But don't worry," Lucy jumped in. "I'm sure we'll get new jobs real soon. Better jobs."

Edith, their middle daughter, scrunched up her nose. "What's better than being super-cool secret agents?"

"Oh, I know!" Agnes cried. "You could gamble online! That's what Katie's dad does!"

"Okay, we will definitely look into that. Good suggestion," Gru said, trying to comfort them. "And let's not go over to Katie's house anymore. . . ."

Just then Gru's cell phone rang. He glanced down, realizing that Mel was calling. He was definitely not looking forward to breaking the news to the Minions. He finished his dinner as slowly as humanly possible and then made his way down to his underground lair.

He stood onstage; the cheering was so loud it hurt his ears. There was a sea of Minions in the audience in front of him, jumping up and down and shrieking with delight. Some of them pulled out their old blasters and weapons.

"Guys, *shhhhhh*," Gru called out. "I don't think you heard me right. No, no, no, no, no, no, this does not mean that we are going back to being villains!"

The Minions froze. They seemed upset.

Mel, the leader of the Minions, marched forward and stared up at Gru.

"Pinouf!" he yelled. "Flaku biko!"

Gru sighed. "Okay, alright, I get it. Look, I know it's been a little tough lately, especially with Doctor Nefario accidentally freezing himself in carbonite—" Gru glanced sadly at Nefario, who was encased in a block of carbonite. A few Minions were still trying to free him with a jackhammer. "—but our life of crime is over!"

Mel directed Gru's attention toward a large screen above the stage. He clicked a button on his remote and images flew past of Gru's old life as a villain. The moment he stole the moon, the moment he defeated Vector, one of his battles with El Macho. Then there were other pictures right next to them: pictures of Gru riding a lawn mower; picking up poo left in the yard by his dog,

Kyle; using a plunger to unclog the toilet—as if his new life were a lot less exciting. The Minions had a small point—he wasn't so fond of cleaning up poo.

"Ahhh, pffft," Mel said. "Looka! Bueno . . . pinouf! Bueno . . . pinouf! Bueno . . . pinouf! Minions . . . no le pinouf!!"

"Pinouf! Pinouf!" the Minions cried, chanting in protest.

"Guys! Listen to me and read my lips!" Gru said. "Lissa me lippo, pomodoro la comquit!"

The Minions burst out laughing. Gru hadn't perfected his Minionese, but he thought he was at least close.

"What? What did I just say?" he asked. "It's not comquit? Okay, pomodoro la kumquat."

Now the Minions just looked confused.

"Whoa, whoa," Mel sneered. "Tudi se comquit para no. No le para yo."

"Don't take that tone with me!" Gru cried. "We're not going back to villainy. And I don't want to hear another word about it."

Gru turned on his heel and headed for the door. But then *PHBBBLT!!!*

There was a loud raspberry sound from the back of the room. Then another one. And another one. All the Minions were mocking him.

"Look, if you guys don't stop that right now, there will be consequences!" Gru yelled.

Mel stepped forward, pointing up at Gru. "Aaargh! Puriquences, mi molo!"

Gru pointed right back at him. "Don't say anything you're going to regret."

"Nori kaboss," Mel yelled, throwing his hat on the ground. "Noori quitas! Ciao bello!"

"What? You quit?" Gru asked. But Mel was already leading all the Minions out the door. "You're serious?"

They stormed out, ignoring Gru. One

of them stomped on Mel's hat. When they were all gone, Gru stared at the lair. He wasn't used to seeing it so empty.

FOOMP! FOOMP!

The transport tubes spat Dave and Jerry into the lair. They were still wearing their Hawaiian gear—grass skirts and all.

"Dave! Jerry!" Gru said. "Great news, guys—you've been promoted. You're in charge now, eh? Not bad!"

Dave and Jerry stared at each other, wondering if they'd heard Gru right. Could it be? Was it really possible that *they'd* be running the show from now on?

They didn't want to give Gru time to question it. They just pulled off their costumes and rubbed their butts together in celebration.

"Yipa! Yipo!" they cheered. "Aruba-ruba-ruba-ruba!"

The two ran off to celebrate, leaving Gru alone. He stared out the window, looking at the moon—the same prize that not so long ago he'd stolen for himself. Were the Minions right? Had his life become too good . . . too *boring*?

■ ■ ■ ■ ■ ■ ● ● ■ ■ ■ ■ ■ ■

"Hey, Gru," Lucy said, glancing around the empty lair. "Whatcha doing down here? In the dark. Alone. You okay?"

Gru rubbed his forehead. He wasn't sure how much time had passed since the Minions left. It could've been hours.

"Oh yes, yes, I'm fine," he said. "It's just . . . I don't know. I guess I just feel like a . . . failure. Like I don't have a purpose anymore."

Gru tried to turn away, but Lucy put her hand on his cheek. She always had a way of making him feel better.

"Hey, mister," she said. "You are not a failure."

"If only I could've nailed Bratt. So many times I almost had him! But now I'll never get the chance. 'Cause I have been kicked to the curb."

"Gru, you've got to let this go," Lucy said, staring into his huge brown eyes. "It's time to look forward. Things will get better."

She kissed him on the cheek. Gru closed his eyes, wanting to believe her, but he couldn't shake a terrible feeling. Maybe this was it for him. Maybe he'd never again do anything worthwhile.

Had Balthazar Bratt been right? Was Gru the world's worst agent?

CHAPTER 5

The next morning, Gru pulled on his robe and went to get the paper. He tried to keep Lucy's words in his head. Things would get better. It was time to look forward. Who was Valerie Da Vinci to think she could end his career? He was so much more than just a secret agent of AVL who saved the world by defeating one evil villain at a time!

He opened the door to find his dog, Kyle, gnawing away on the paper. Then he saw the headline.

"No, no—you've got to be kidding me," Gru said. The Dupont Diamond was supposed to be safe in a guarded museum in Paris. They told him Balthazar Bratt would never be able to get to it, no matter how hard he tried.

"Lucy, did you see—" Gru started, but he got distracted by Agnes. Agnes had set up a table on the sidewalk, and Dave and Jerry were helping her sell all her worldly possessions: toys, books, a vacuum cleaner, and even some pots and pans from the kitchen.

Agnes handed her stuffed unicorn to a little girl. "He helps you if you have nightmares, and he's really good to snuggle with—"

"Oh no, no, no, Agnes!" Gru cried, running toward her.

"So take good care of him," Agnes said as the little girl took off down the street.

"Agnes," Gru said, stooping down beside her. "What are you doing? You sold your unicorn?"

"Well, I just wanted to help." Agnes shrugged. "Since you don't have a job. I got two whole dollars for it!"

"Awwwww," Dave and Jerry cooed.

A well-dressed man walked toward them, stopping in front of Agnes's table.

"Sorry, buddy—sale's over."

"But this will only take a—"

"Hey, Eyebrows!" Gru yelled. "Get off the lawn."

But the man was still standing there, staring at them as if he had something to say. Gru thrust a vacuum cleaner into the man's hands and pressed the button on the front.

TCHOOOM!

The vacuum took off like a rocket, launching the man down the street. Gru laughed and then turned back to Agnes.

"Listen, Agnes," he said sweetly. "You don't need to worry. We're going to be fine."

Agnes stared up at him with her big brown eyes. "For real?"

"For real. Now come on, let's pack this stuff up." He stooped down, picked up a teddy bear and some dolls Agnes loved, and put them back into a box. He was about to put away the dollhouse when he noticed the man coming back. He was limping and a little tattered-looking, but he actually had the nerve to come back.

"Seriously?" Gru asked. "Buddy, you're not getting the hint."

"Ow, ow," the man said, his leg obviously hurt. "Allow me to introduce myself—my name is Fritz, and *OW!*"

Gru looked down, realizing that Kyle was biting his leg. But even that didn't stop Fritz from continuing.

"And I am inquiring . . . good puppy . . . on behalf of your twin brother, Dru."

"What? Twin brother?" Gru asked.

"Yes," Fritz said. "He would like to fly you to Freedonia to meet him. Your father has recently passed away and—"

"Okay, cuckoo," Gru said, twirling his finger next to his head like Fritz was nuts. "I'm sorry, but my dad died when I was a baby, and I don't have any brother. You've got the wrong guy."

Gru grabbed a box and started walking away, gesturing for Agnes and the Minions to follow.

"Really?" Fritz asked. "Well, then how do you explain this?"

He shoved an old, wrinkled photo

underneath Gru's nose. It was clearly Gru's mom. She was a little younger and seemed a little kinder, but she was holding two identical twin boys. They both looked just like Gru.

Gru grabbed it from Fritz's hand, unsure what to believe. Was that really him? And did he really have a twin brother his mom had never told him about?

CHAPTER 6

Gru had decided to go directly to the source.

When he showed up at his mother's palatial mansion, she was in the swimming pool, doing the backstroke with some handsome diving instructors. She had on her most flattering vintage one-piece, and she'd traded her signature red glasses for swimming goggles.

"*Ahhhhh! Bellissimo!*" one with massive biceps cooed. His hands were under the water. Gru thought he was holding up her back, but he couldn't be sure.

"Oh, hello, Gru!" she said, giggling like a schoolgirl.

"Hi, Mom . . . ," Gru's relationship with his mother had always been hard, to say the least. How many times can your mother tell you you're a failure before it starts to sting a bit?

"It's important to keep active in one's golden years," Gru's mom said as another handsome man popped up beside her. "These are my diving instructors, Vincenzo and Paolo! Ciao, boys!"

The diving instructors obeyed and left Gru and his mom alone. She turned to Gru and asked, "So what do you want?"

Gru stared at his mom, unsure of how to delicately ask his question.

"Mom, do I have a twin brother?" he finally blurted out.

Gru's mom stared at him, stunned. "How did you find out? Who told you?"

"Wait, what? It's true?" Gru asked. "You never told me I had a brother! And you told me that Dad died of disappointment when I was born!"

That was true. She really did tell him that.

His mom waved her hand at him. "Yeah, yeah, that was the agreement."

"Agreement? What are you talking about?"

Gru's mom plucked the old photograph from Gru's hand and stared at it. She let out a deep sigh. "Shortly after you and your brother were born, your father and I divorced. We each took one son to raise on our own. And promised never to see each other again."

She crumpled up the photo in her hand and then passed it back to Gru.

"Obviously, I got second pick," she grumbled.

She turned and went back into the house, not bothering to say anything else. Gru pressed the crumpled photo flat, smoothing it down on his leg. He stared at it a second time.

The boys looked exactly alike. They had the same big brown eyes, the same long, hooked nose. They were even wearing the same outfit.

"I have a brother . . . ," he said, letting the fact sink in. He had a brother.

He tucked the photo back in his pocket and smiled.

CHAPTER 7

While Gru packed his bags for Freedonia, the Minions were on their own adventure. Mel and the Minions marched through the city. But after a while, they were tired, cold, and hungry. The Minions began to murmur and turn on their leader.

As they paraded through the streets of Los Angeles, Mel tried to keep them happy. He spotted a pizza truck and ordered the Minions to follow it.

"Pizza! Pizza! Pizza!" the Minions chanted

as they raced toward the truck. They charged through a pair of security gates that marked the entrance to a movie studio backlot. They didn't notice the guards screaming at them. They kept going, stopping only when they'd reached the pizza truck. They started grabbing all the boxes!

"There they are!" a security guard yelled. He called for backup, and soon a handful of guards arrived to try to stop the Minions. "Hey, you! Don't move! Stop right there!"

The Minions scattered. Dozens ran into a soundstage, trying to escape. They made their way down a long, dark hallway, toward some bright lights. They turned a corner, and suddenly they were onstage, the spotlights shining down on them. Three celebrity judges sat behind a desk. It was some sort of talent show!

One of the judges pressed a button, and the microphone in front of the Minions lowered to their height. Music started playing in the background. It was their time to shine.

A Minion pushed Mel forward. He began singing a soulful song from one of his favorite musicals, *The Pirates of Penzance*. The Minions all joined in as more security guards rushed the stage.

"Get 'em!" one guard yelled. "Go! Go!"

But the group of Minions was determined to show off their talents. If Mel got to sing, why couldn't they perform, too? They started doing the cancan. They lifted up their skirts, revealing smiley faces painted on their behinds.

The audience went crazy. The judges stood up, giving the Minions a standing ovation, but the security guards were less impressed.

"Hands in the air!" they yelled, surrounding the stage.

Mel spotted them, and his face fell. He knew this was it—they'd been caught.

"Uh-oh . . . ," he mumbled.

CHAPTER 8

■■■■■■■■■■

Gru stared out the window of the private jet. The sun was shining, and there wasn't a cloud in sight. It seemed like a sign that what Lucy had said was true—things would get better. And sooner than he had thought.

"I wonder what Dru will be like!" Gru said, drumming his fingers on his leg. "Maybe we'll have that twin thing where we can read each other's minds. How cool would that be?!"

"Um, super cool!" Lucy said.

The parachute in the top of the plane exploded open, letting the jet ease toward the ground. They touched down in the middle of the ocean on a runway covered with pigs. Big, fat, pink pigs, running and squealing in all directions.

"Woo-hoo! Freedonia!" the girls cried as the jet sped toward a beautiful mansion with a pink roof. The rolling hills behind it were covered with cypress and olive trees.

The girls ran off the jet. Several pigs approached them, oinking in greeting.

"Hi, piggy, piggy!" Agnes said, chasing one in circles.

"Whoa, look at that house!" Edith pointed to the giant mansion. It was covered in ornate gold accents that sparkled in the sun. The walkway to it was lined with white marble columns, each one with a pig sculpture on top.

"It's like a castle!" Agnes said.

Gru dragged everyone's suitcases off the plane, trying not to bump his head on the way out. He stepped down and took a deep breath, smelling the ocean air . . . and something foul. "What's with all the pigs?"

Fritz appeared behind him. "This is the family business," he said. "The largest pig farm in the whole of Freedonia!"

As he said it, a huge, ugly pig ran up to Gru, nudging him in the butt.

"Okay, nice pig," Gru tried. But the pig just nudged him harder. "No! That's my private part!"

He started running, but the pig followed. They ran all the way to the front door of the mansion, and Gru didn't dare stop until he was safely inside. He slammed the door behind him, trying to catch his breath.

The mansion was even more impressive inside. It seemed as if every surface was decorated with a pig theme. Two pink velvet armchairs had snouts and eyes. The bookcase had pig ears, and every column and railing was topped with a carved pink pig. There were even two dancing pig sculptures at the top of the stairs.

"Oh, this is amazing!" Lucy said, gazing at the mural on the ceiling. "It's like the Sistine Chapel. But with pigs."

They were so busy staring at the beautiful architecture that they barely noticed the man coming down the staircase.

"My brother!!" Dru called out, opening his arms wide.

He was dressed head to toe in white, with a white fedora and sunglasses. He was smiling, a big genuine smile, and seemed to have the confidence and personality Gru had always hoped for.

"Gru!" he said as he got closer.

"Dru!" Gru said, thrilled. Not only did he have a brother, but the brother looked exactly like him. They were mirror images of each other.

But then, with a flick of his wrist, Dru took off his hat. His mop of golden hair cascaded down onto his shoulders. Gru's smiled faded. He couldn't stop staring. It was so thick . . . so lustrous. The hair of angels, or catalog models, or the boys on the playground who made fun of Gru when he was small. It was simply . . . beautiful.

"Ahhhh!" Dru hugged Gru tight. "Brother! I am hugging you! I'm so happy!"

Gru stood there awkwardly, not quite sure what to do with his arms. Dru was hugging him so hard he'd picked him up off the ground. Dru grabbed Gru's scarf with both hands, pressing his cheek against Gru's. Gru squirmed, a bit uncomfortable with the affection.

"After all these years, finally I'm meeting you!"

"Yup, good," Gru said, wondering when he could get away.

Dru turned, noticing Lucy and the girls.

"Oh, look at that! You must be the beautiful wife!" he said. "How is my brother finding a wife like you when he is so bald?"

Dru rubbed Gru's head as if he were polishing a bowling ball. Then he turned, grabbing Gru's shoulders. "I'm joking!" He laughed. "Who doesn't love this guy? Look at him!" Gru almost smiled, but then Dru added, "Oh, but hair would make you better."

Dru laughed again and then playfully punched Gru in the stomach. As he started tickling his sides, Gru tried to appear calm. In actuality, he wanted to sock Dru right in the nose.

"I wanna tickle you!" Dru laughed. "I wanna tickle you!"

The girls laughed right along with him.

"These must be my nieces!" Dru turned to them. "You're Agnes—you are small with big eyes. And it makes me want to put you in my pocket! And Edith—I can tell that you are a little mischievous. We're gonna have to make a little trouble later."

"I already have . . . ," Edith said. She'd taped a KICK ME sign to Fritz's back, and now Dave and Jerry were both kicking him in the shins.

"Fist bump for mischievous behavior!" Dru said, bumping his knuckles against Edith's. "And Margo! Oh, you are so mature. I'm guessing what . . . fifteen?"

"She's twelve!" Gru snapped. "She looks twelve. She will always be twelve."

"Your discomfort is hilarious." Dru laughed. "Oh man, having a brother is the best! What could be better than this?"

He punched Gru in the stomach again, just for fun.

"I dunno . . . ," Gru grumbled. "Never having met you?"

"I love your sense of humor," Dru went on. "It's funny because it's not true!"

Lucy must've noticed how annoyed Gru was because she took a step into the great hall. "So, Dru . . . this place is amazing. I mean, you just walk through the doors and you're like: *wooooowwwooowwooooo!!*"

Dru's face grew serious. "Eh. It's nice, I guess, sure. I'm not really into 'things.'"

Then he flung open some nearby doors, revealing a row of expensive cars.

"This is so cool!" Edith said. "Oh my gosh, he's even got a helicopter!"

Gru couldn't help himself—he had to look. Sure enough, there was a giant red helicopter sitting right next to one of Dru's fanciest cars. It seemed brand-new.

"This is the best!" Agnes said, jumping up and down.

Gru slowed his pace so he was walking beside Lucy. They let the girls go ahead with Dru.

"Yes, the best," Gru managed to say. "All right, let's go home now."

"Home? Why?" Lucy asked.

"I don't know, this guy, with the mansion and the cars and . . . all the hair," Gru moaned. "Silky-smooth, luxurious hair. I feel worse than I did before I came."

Lucy gave Gru a sympathetic nod. Of course Dru made Gru feel bad about himself. The fancy cars, and the giant mansion, and the private plane . . . all after they'd just lost their jobs working for AVL. Poor Agnes had been selling her belongings on the street.

But they were there already, weren't they? And Dru was family, wasn't he? How could they fly back now?

"He's your brother, Gru," Lucy said, as if that settled it. "Give him a chance."

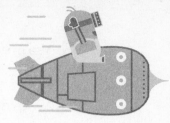

CHAPTER 9

Gru and Dru strolled through the grounds behind the mansion. They followed Dave and Jerry, who were running up to every pig they saw and getting right in its snout.

"*Ooooo*, piggy, piggy!" Dave yelled at a piglet.

Fritz had taken Lucy and the girls on a tour of Freedonia so Gru and Dru could have some alone time. Now they were walking and talking . . . alone. Gru was so uncomfortable that he wanted to ride one of the pigs off into the sunset.

"So how are things going for you, career-wise?" Dru asked.

Gru smiled as big as he could. *"Ahhaaaaa . . .* great. So, so great. Crushing it."

"Well, I've got something that I think you will find very interesting. Hold on to your face, Brother," said Dru.

Dru stopped in front of a stone statue of a pig. He stuck his finger into the pig's snout and a remote control popped out. Then he punched a code into it and grabbed Gru's hand. The ground beneath them dropped a few inches. Dru looked down, disappointed. Clearly something else was supposed to happen.

He jumped up and down, stomping on the platform beneath them until the trapdoor gave way. Gru and Dru plummeted into an underground lair.

"Aaaahhhhhhh!" Gru screamed, his stomach dropping. *"Whaaaaaaaaaa!"*

The Minions dove in behind them, riding their new friend—a huge pink pig—and carrying its little piglet in their arms. They all fell several stories until a massive fan at the bottom slowed their speed. Dru floated for a moment and then landed gracefully. Gru fell flat on his head.

Thunk! Boof!

Dave and Jerry weren't far behind. Dave reached up, catching the piglet just in time. Jerry raised his arms, preparing to catch the pig, but it smushed him flat.

"Le salami!" Dave cried.

"Come on, come on," Dru said, waving Gru over. He strode down a long hallway lined with statues of Gru family villains. Dru wrapped his arm around his brother.

"What is all this?" Gru asked, noticing a statue that looked a lot like him, if he were six inches shorter.

"The pig farm was just a cover for the real family business," Dru said.

"Haha!" Dave pointed to a statue of a woman villain. "C'est Gru con boobs!"

Dru stopped in front of the door at the end of the hall. "Now, feast your eyes on . . ." He pressed a button and the door opened, revealing one of the most sophisticated lairs Gru had ever seen. There were dozens of high-tech computers, holograms, weapons, and gadgets. "Dad's lair! Ta-da!"

"Whoa whoa whoa, wait . . . ," Gru said, taking it all in. "So our dad was a villain?"

"Not just a villain!" Dru said. "But one of the greatest of all time!"

Gru turned, looking up at an oil painting of a man with his face. There were so many similarities—they had the same eyes, the same long, hooked nose. And unlike Dru, his father was also bald.

"That's him?" Gru asked. "That's our dad?"

"He was so proud of you," said Dru. "And what a great villain you were."

"He was?" asked Gru, surprised.

Dru nodded. "But me . . . not so much." He took a longing look at the portrait of their father. "To Dad, I was just a failure. He never thought I had what it took to be a villain."

Dru paused for a moment and looked to his brother. "But now you can help me prove him wrong. Brother, teach me the art of villainy!"

Dru leaned in close and raised an eyebrow.

"No. No, no, no," Gru said. "I can't do that."

"What? But it's our family tradition! You can't say no to that!"

Gru shook his head solemnly. "Look, I'm

sorry. I've left that life behind me. End of story."

Dru let out a deep sigh. His shoulders slumped. It was the most upset Gru had seen him all day.

"Oh, okay. I understand," Dru said sadly. Then he turned to a lever on the wall. "*Hmmm* . . . I wonder what this does?"

He pulled the lever and the floor opened up; Dave, Jerry, and the pigs all fell below. Within seconds, an amazing villain vehicle, a cross between a Lamborghini and a spaceship, popped up. It was gold, with two red leather seats and a turbo blaster on the back. Dave, Jerry, and the pigs were all squished inside.

Gru took a few steps toward it, amazed.

"Dad's villain wheels. Pretty slick, huh?" Dru stepped closer, whispering in Gru's ear. "Want to take her out for a spin? Just for some fun?"

Then Dru spread out on the hood of the car. He smiled his most mischievous smile.

Gru looked at him, then at the car, then back at him.

"*Hmmmmm . . . ,*" Gru mused, considering it.

Just one ride, just for a few minutes. Was there any harm in that?

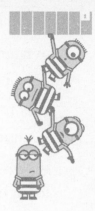

CHAPTER 10

Their little stunt on the reality show cost the Minions their freedom. The Minions were promptly rounded up and thrown in jail with some of the most hardened criminals.

But if those criminals were hard ... the Minions were harder. Mel ruled the roost, finally becoming the villain he'd always dreamed of being. The Minions had food fights. They snapped wet towels at other inmates when they tried to take their showers. But no matter how powerful Mel became, no matter how much he was feared, he couldn't help but feel a hole in his heart. Something was missing, and that something was Gru.

One day, when he was eating his lumpy mashed potatoes, he sculpted them so they looked like Gru. He stared at the image of Gru, missing his former boss.

Mel decided then: He'd find Gru. They'd go back to him, even if he wasn't so villainous anymore. That's when Mel came up with his plan. . . .

CHAPTER 11

Welcome to the annual Freedonian Cheese Festival!" Fritz called out.

The village square was filled with people. A man threw cheese daggers at a woman on a spinning wheel. Another villager tossed colorful hoops at bottles, trying to win the carnival game. A line of villagers passed Lucy and the girls, singing a song they didn't recognize.

Agnes and Edith ran to a booth at the side of the road. The man was selling giant lollipops, candy bars, and caramels wrapped in shiny foil. Edith grabbed a lollipop and held it high in the air.

"Lucy, can we get these?" she asked.

"Okay, but only one each. I mean it," Lucy said, taking out her wallet. She paused before handing the girls a wad of cash. "No, I don't! Get as many as you want, I don't care!"

"Yay!" the girls cheered. They ran to the booth and bought fistfuls of candy.

Margo sighed.

"What?" Lucy asked.

"It's okay to tell them no sometimes, too, you know," she said. "Moms need to be tough."

Lucy nodded. "Right, tough. I can totally do that. You know, still figuring out this mom thing. Getting my sea legs!"

Just then Agnes spotted a store with a unicorn out front. Only it wasn't a store . . .

it was a bar called the Tipsy Unicorn. That didn't matter to her, though.

"A unicorn!" she cried. "Can we go in there! Please please please? *Please???*"

Lucy looked at the pub. Suddenly the doors flung open, and two burly guys flew out, wrestling each other to the ground. "Um, sure . . . ," she said. "But first, let's, um . . . *ooh*, look! It's a traditional Freedonian dance! How amazing does that look?"

Just a little farther up the road, there was a group of boys and girls around Margo's age. They wore traditional Freedonian garb. The boys all held trays with wedges of cheese on them. One by one the girls approached the boys, took a bite of their cheese, and the crowd cheered. Each pair walked off together.

"Oh no, look at that poor little guy," Lucy said, staring at the one boy who was left onstage. "With his little boots. Nobody picked him. Margo, why don't you go up there?"

"No way!" Margo said, backing up.

"Okay," Lucy agreed. But then she realized . . . this was her chance to be firm. Moms needed to be tough. "No—go take a bite of his cheese, young lady. Right now."

"What?" Margo's eyes were wide.

"Oh, come on, just do it," Lucy said. "What's the worst that could happen?"

Margo stared at the little boy onstage and sighed. Lucy was right—he looked miserable. She trudged up the stairs and introduced herself, and he told her his name was Niko. Then she took a bite of his cheese.

"*Hmmm* . . . ," she said, chewing.

"Yes, yes, yes!" Niko cried. "Thank you, Margo! *Woo-hooo!* Margo, you have made me the happiest man in Freedonia!"

Niko's family rushed around him and cheered.

"BAM!" Lucy yelled. "I am a great mother! Did you see that, girls?"

She turned, waiting for Edith and Agnes to respond, but they weren't there. She glanced around. They weren't anywhere.

"Oh no . . . ," Lucy said, panicking. "Agnes! Edith!"

Gru was once a super villain. Now he's a super spy working for the Anti-Villain League (AVL).

But that doesn't last long. Gru and his wife, Lucy, are fired by Valerie Di Vinci, the new head of the AVL, after they accidentally let the villainous Balthazar Bratt escape.

Back at home, Margo, Edith, and Agnes surprise
Gru and Lucy with a luau for their honeymoon.

Two Minions, Dave and Jerry, play their ukuleles.
But even the Minions are upset that Gru and Lucy
were fired.

Agnes is worried about her parents, so she decides to sell her favorite things in a yard sale. She even sells her fluffy unicorn to a neighbor for two dollars.

Just when things are looking really bad for Gru, he learns that he has a secret twin brother named Dru! Dru wants Gru to visit him in Freedonia, so the entire family takes a ride on a private plane—all the way to Dru's mansion.

It turns out Dru wishes he could be a super villain, just like Gru was!

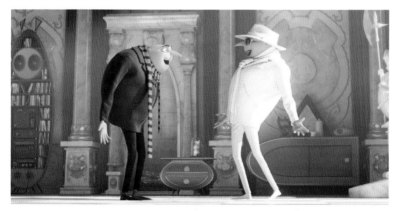

When Dru steals two lollipops, they get into a high-speed chase with the Freedonian pig-riding police.

The chase brings them all the way back to Dru's home, where Gru, Dru, the Minions (and their pigs) go through a trapdoor to a secret lair.

 **What could be inside?**

Meanwhile, Agnes spots a pub called the Tipsy Unicorn. There, she and Edith meet a man who says that unicorns are *real*—and Agnes can find one in the Crooked Forest!

Will Agnes's dream finally come true?

CHAPTER 12

"Look!" Agnes cried as she ran through the pub. She pointed up at a mounted horn on the wall. "A unicorn horn! My little brain is going to explode!"

Edith rolled her eyes. "Ugh, Agnes. That's a fake."

Agnes stared at the horn, her smile falling.

"*Ohhhh*, it's real alright," a voice said behind them.

A burly man put a drink down in front of a customer, then leaned over the bar, smiling at the little girls. "That horn came from the Crooked Forest. The only place on earth where unicorns still live."

A couple at one of the tables started laughing. Another man snickered as he threw a dart. It seemed as if all the villagers had heard this story before.

"Go on, laugh!" the bartender said. "Laugh, all of you! They all think I'm crazy. But I'm telling you, I saw one once. With my own eye!"

Agnes stared up at the man, completely enthralled. "Wait, wait, wait . . . ," she said. "You saw a for-real, live unicorn? What did it look like? Did you pet it? Did it smell like candy? Was it . . . fluffy?"

"It was so fluffy I thought I was going to die," the bartender said.

"Do you think maybe I could find one, too?" Agnes asked.

The man nodded. "They say if a maiden

pure of heart goes into the Crooked Forest, the unicorn will come . . . and be hers forever."

Agnes couldn't take it anymore. A real, live unicorn that she could take home as a pet? She squealed in excitement, her shriek filling the entire pub.

Just then Lucy busted through the doors with a high kick. She made her way through the crowd, kicking and punching patrons as she went. A chubby, bearded man took a boot to the face. She threw another man into an arcade game. She lifted a table and smashed it down on two villagers' heads. Then she grabbed the handles on a foosball table and slammed them into a man's gut.

"Goal!" she yelled.

She was so pumped up it took her a moment to remember where she was. She spotted Agnes and Edith across the room. "Girls! Don't worry, I'm here!"

She grabbed Agnes, hugging the girl to her chest. "Are you okay?" she asked.

"We're fine—are *you*?" Edith eyed Lucy as if she were insane.

Agnes looked at Lucy, grinning.

"Unicorns are really real! And I'm gonna find one!!" she said, pointing to the unicorn horn mounted on the pub wall.

Agnes ran out of the pub, still yelling in excitement. Lucy grabbed Edith's hand, finally realizing the havoc she'd caused. There were people strewn all over the floor. A grown man was sobbing loudly, his face in his hands.

"Sorry I went a little mama bear on you," she said, backing out the door. "You know, I heard a scream and . . . yeah, okay. Have a good one!"

She smiled and waved, trying to sound as cheerful as possible. Then they rushed off to find Fritz.

CHAPTER 13

◀◀◀◀◀◀◀◀◀◀◀◀◀

Zero to four hundred in three seconds!"
Dru yelled over the sound of the engine.
"Able to withstand a nuclear blast, armed
to the teeth!"

He pushed a button on the dashboard and
dozens of guns, bombs, and spikes popped
out of the car from all sides. Gru stared at
them in awe.

"Okay, that's pretty nice," Gru admitted.
He could barely move. They were going
so fast his whole body was glued to the

seat, his cheeks blown back by the force. Dru turned the corner, and a tractor was coming right at them. He smashed through a roadblock, and the car flew off a cliff. They were in free fall, plummeting down to the ocean.

"*Ahhhh!!*" Gru screamed, seeing his life flash before his eyes: tucking Agnes into bed, playing with little kitten finger puppets, watching the girls dancing in their tutus. Lucy.

Dru hit another button on the dash. Two grappling hooks flew out of the front of the car, metal cables spiraling behind them. They dug into the cliff's edge, and the car swung down, its tires landing against the rock. Dru slammed on the gas, and the car drove right up the rock wall and back onto the road.

"Help me!" Gru screamed, his eyes only half open.

Dru didn't seem to notice. He kept going just as fast until they approached a village. The car screeched to a stop.

"Wait for me here!" Dru called as he hopped out. He ran over to a candy truck that was parked on the side of the road. A sign on the door read CLOSED DUE TO CHEESE FESTIVAL. Dru picked the lock and went inside. Seconds later an alarm sounded, and Dru emerged with two huge lollipops. He pushed Gru into the driver's seat.

"Did you just steal candies?" Gru asked.

"Yes!" Dru said cheerfully.

"That was a lot of effort for two lollipops."

"But they're the best in Freedonia!" Dru cried, shoving one in Gru's mouth.

Sirens sounded in the distance. Gru sat there, chewing on his lollipop.

"The police!" Dru cried, nudging him. "What do we do?"

Gru hit the accelerator, and the car sped off. The police appeared behind them, lights flashing, but Gru was going so fast they couldn't keep up. He laughed and laughed, remembering how good it felt to be bad.

"The police are going to get us! I'm freaking out!" Dru said, panicking.

Gru kept driving until they came to a pig herder, whose pigs were blocking the middle of the road. Gru slammed on the brakes, and the car skidded to a stop just inches from a pig's head. The Freedonian police were right behind them, though, approaching on their bikes.

"Cops!" Dru cried.

Gru pushed a button, and the car raised up, letting the police bikes pass underneath them. They rode straight into the herd of pigs. The bikes flew one way, and the policemen flew the other. Gru lowered the car and continued on.

But when he looked in the rearview mirror, he saw the police were still after them— now they were riding the pigs like horses. A blind man crossed the street up ahead. If they stopped for him, they'd be caught.

Gru hit another button, and the car burrowed underground, driving through the city wall until the vehicle broke through to the ocean. They flew into the sea and disappeared into the water below, the car transforming into a submarine. Gru kept going, not taking his foot off the gas until he was sure they were safe.

"Man, that was crazy!" Dru laughed. "We were so close to getting busted!"

"Tell me about it," Gru said. "I thought you were going to pee your pants!"

"I did!!" Dru laughed again.

They drove the car underwater, Dru directing Gru to a beach that was close to his mansion. The two went ashore and wrung out their clothes. Dru hung them up on a nearby clothesline as Gru stretched out in the sun, feeling better than he had in days.

"Face it, Gru," Dru said. "Villainy is in your blood. You can't tell me you don't miss the rush. A little?"

"Well . . ." Gru couldn't help but smile. "Maybe a little."

Dru lay down next to his brother, tucking his hands behind his head.

"And now you've got a chance to get back on top," Dru said. "Get your mojo back. Become Gru again! How awesome would that be? Oh please, come on, just one heist. There's got to be something out there, somewhere, that you still want to steal."

Gru closed his eyes. He could see himself, standing before a cheering crowd, holding the Dupont Diamond. Valerie Da Vinci would tell him that she had been rude, that she had been so, so rude and so, so wrong. Lucy would look at him with admiration, and Balthazar Bratt would be stuck in a gum trap, whining about how horrible it was that Gru had outsmarted him.

"*Hmmmm* . . . ," Gru said. "There is something. How about we steal the largest diamond in the world?"

"Yes! I love it!" Dru cried. "Oh, thank you, Brother! Thank you from the bottom of my heart!"

They both ran out into the ocean, dancing. They jumped up and down and hugged as the waves rolled in around them.

"Oh! You know what?" Dru asked. "We should do something to celebrate."

Gru stared at Dru's thick mop of blond hair and smiled.

"*Ohhhh,*" he said. "I've got the perfect idea. . . ."

CHAPTER 14

///////////////////////

Gru and Dru strode into the dining room, trying to keep their faces straight. Gru could barely look at his brother. Dru was wearing a bald cap and the black jacket and striped scarf that Gru usually wore. Gru was dressed like Dru—an all-white suit with this silly blond wig that kept falling in his eyes.

"Here we are!" Gru announced, looking at Lucy and the girls. They were sitting at the table with Fritz and Kyle.

"How's it going?" Dru tried to make his voice more Gru-like. "It's me, Gru!"

The two brothers sat down at the table. Lucy and the girls didn't look amused, but that didn't stop the brothers.

"What's for dinner?" Dru asked. "I probably won't like it. I'm so grumpy all the time!"

"Hey! I laugh a lot!" Gru smiled. "And I'm kind of an idiot!"

Gru and Dru glanced sideways at each other. They couldn't take it anymore. They both broke into laughter.

"Look at them!" Dru cried. "They had no idea."

Gru removed his wig. "Look, it's me—Gru!"

Dru pulled off his bald cap. "And I'm Dru! We switched places!"

Margo and Lucy seemed unimpressed. Then Lucy offered a small smile.

"It's so nice to see you two are getting along," Lucy said.

"Oh, we're getting—" Gru started.

"Along perfectly," Dru finished.

The brothers turned to each other.

"Wait," Gru said. "Did we—"

"Just finish—"

"Each—"

"Other's—"

"Sentences?" they said together.

"Aw, that's delightful," Lucy said. "Not creepy at all. And you're gonna stop, though, now, right?"

"Sorry," Gru said. "It's a twin thing."

"So what did you guys do today?" Lucy asked.

"Nothing!" Gru and Dru said in unison.

Lucy stared at them. Something was up . . . but what?

"All done!" Agnes said, interrupting them. She hopped off her chair and started upstairs to the guest room. "Pardon me! Out of the way! Good night, everybody!"

She pushed past Fritz, who nearly dropped their fish dinner on the floor.

"Hey, put the brakes on," Gru said. "What's the rush?"

"I need to go to bed so I can wake up and find a unicorn!" Agnes said. "Good night!"

Gru watched her go, completely confused.

"Agnes thinks she's going to find a real unicorn in the woods tomorrow," Edith explained. "She's totally freaking out."

Lucy shook her head. "I feel like someone has to tell her the truth. . . . Not it!"

Everyone at the table turned to look at Gru. Maybe it wasn't fair, but he was the best man for the job. Who else would Agnes listen to?

"Don't worry," Gru said before heading upstairs to find Agnes. "Parenting 101. I've got this."

By the time he got to the guest room, Agnes

was in the middle of her good-night prayer. "*Ummm . . . ,*" she said. "And please bless that when I find the unicorn, he'll want to come home with me. And sleep in my room. And that I can ride him to school every day. And he will use his magical powers to help me do math. Amen."

"So . . . big day tomorrow," Gru said.

"I'm finally going to get to see a unicorn! For reals," Agnes said. "If I do, can I bring it home, please?"

"Tell you what," Gru said, choosing his words carefully. "Every unicorn you find, you can bring it home. I'd better build a big pen, right? But you know . . . there's a chance that you might not find one."

"Huh?" Agnes said. Her brows furrowed.

"They're tricky to find them . . . and I don't know . . ." Gru tried to find the right thing to say. "Maybe, just—maybe unicorns don't really ex—"

Agnes's smile fell. She stared at Gru intensely, scared of what he'd say next.

"—explore that part of the woods," he went on.

"But the man said a maiden could find one if she was pure of heart," Agnes said, pulling the blankets up to her chin. "And I'm pure of heart, right?"

Gru's heart swelled.

"The purest," he said, smiling.

"Can we stop talking?" Agnes said. "I need to get to sleep."

Agnes rolled over and started singing to herself.

Sure, Gru hadn't really told her the truth. But what was he supposed to say? No, Agnes, your dreams will never come true? Stop wishing and thinking and hoping to meet a unicorn—it is not going to happen. Ever.

No, Gru wouldn't say that. He'd been mean in the past, but he could never be mean to his Agnes. He turned to leave, fell from the huge ladder that led to her bed, and then stumbled back up to his feet.

CHAPTER 15

Gru stood at Dru's state-of-the-art chalk-board, in front of a simple diagram of Balthazar Bratt's lair. The place was a thin pyramid in the middle of the ocean with a giant Rubik's Cube on top. Gru had been there before, and he remembered the tower and some of the weapons that protected it. Dru sat behind him, sipping coffee out of a #1 BROTHER mug. Occasionally he raised his hand for Fritz to give him a refill.

"Okay." Gru tapped the chalk on the board.

"This is Bratt's lair. It may not look like much, but this place is armed with some of the most high-tech weaponry known to man. It's considered impenetrable."

"But a piece of cake for us, right, Brother?" Dru asked.

"This is not like stealing lollipops. . . ."

Gru hit a button on the side of the board, transforming the diagram into a 3-D view of the lair. Dru grabbed a bowl of popcorn from the table and started chomping fistfuls of it. "Whoa!"

Gru drew missiles and guns popping out of the side of the tower. The diagram zoomed out to reveal fighter planes coming toward it from either side. The fighter planes were destroyed in just two shots.

"This security system can detect an air assault from any direction," Gru explained. "So we'll have to approach low and close to the water."

Gru drew a motorboat with a man inside. The chalkboard animated it, showing it racing through the ocean below Bratt's lair. The man seemed happy—confident even.

"Then there are these deadly spikes," Gru said, pointing to a set of spikes that popped out of the water. "Even if they don't impale you, the poison will do significant damage."

Suddenly the man was ejected from the boat. He hit a spike with full force, and his whole body exploded. "Geronimo!" he yelled as his head floated away. "Ouch!"

Dru stopped eating his popcorn.

"Good to know," he said.

"So here's the plan," Gru went on. "You're the getaway driver. So you'll wait in the boat."

"Wait, hold on." Dru frowned. "Wait in the boat? But I want in on the action!"

"Dru . . . ," Gru started, trying to find the perfect way to spin it. "The getaway driver is the most crucial part of any plan. Do you know how hard it is doing nothing, touching nothing, with all of the adrenaline coursing through your veins . . . and you must wait. Can I count on you?"

Gru stared at Dru, hoping what he'd said had sunk in. *Nothing.* Do nothing. Touch nothing. *Absolutely* nothing. He couldn't risk Dru messing things up.

His brother crossed his arms over his chest. "I guess so . . ."

"So I'll climb up the cube and enter here," Gru said, drawing an arrow to the Rubik's Cube. "Then once I'm inside, somehow I'll find the diamond. I've underestimated Bratt before. This is not going to be easy."

"I think we can handle it." Dru smiled. He leaned forward, pushing a button on the table. Two action suits popped up. "Dad's villain suits!"

Gru and Dru ran over and pulled them on. The suits covered their entire bodies except for their mouths and eyes. Gru's was pitch-black with gold piping along the seams. Dru's was identical, except it was white.

"It's go time!" Gru announced.

CHAPTER 16

"Gru la poyak! Gru la cogaf! Go, go, go! Eh, Peter—c'est pa la!" Mel said to the Minions around him.

They responded, "Ah, okay! Okay!"

The Minions walked through the prison, searching for anything they could use. They caused mayhem everywhere they went. One Minion stole a fan from a security guard's office. Toilets seemed to "walk" their way out of bathroom stalls—one with a man still occupying it.

They had gathered supplies to build a machine for their escape. Now it was time to piece it together. Three Minions flipped over a bathtub, while another screwed a toilet into a platform. The area was being monitored by a security camera. Minions walked away, hidden inside a washing machine, followed by Minions inside other large objects. They froze in place when the camera looked at them and continued onward once it began scanning again.

The Minions worked together to create a flying machine. One of them was electrocuted, which made his eyes glow through his goggles like headlights. Minions stole laundry baskets and sewed together their prison uniforms to create a big sail; they used the light-up Minion as a lamp.

The Minions lifted a dryer into the machine. Finally, the flying machine was assembled. They were ready.

"Bello! Bello! Bello!" the Minion dressed as a flight attendant said, welcoming the passengers who climbed aboard the flying machine. Then the Minion gave the safety instructions. "Pull le mikola mi coden. Pursoo le mikodela—" he said, but before he could finish, his life vest inflated so big he couldn't finish his speech.

Mel started the engine and lifted the sails. Another Minion guided the ship to take off, running along behind it; but then the flying machine lifted up into the air, leaving him behind in the prison yard.

Mel stared out at the sky in front of them. It was finally happening—they were on their way back to their leader.

CHAPTER 17

■●▲●●▲●▲●●▲■

Edith tried to keep the camcorder steady. She panned across the Crooked Forest, past the trees and rocks and mountains.

"Here we are," she said, "in the dark and creepy Crooked Forest, in search of the mythical unicorn. For some reason."

She panned over to Agnes, who was marching in front of her, scanning the trees for any signs of the unicorn. "And here she is," Edith went on, "our fearless unicorn hunter, seeking the—"

"Stop it!" Agnes said. "You're gonna scare away the unicorn!"

"If somehow we actually find a unicorn, I'm gonna film it and get rich," Edith said.

"Over there!" Agnes said, pointing to a clearing a few yards off. A pillar of sunlight cut through the canopy of trees. There was a small, grassy hill, and a pond with a waterfall. A rainbow spread across the sky. It looked like something out of a fairy tale.

Agnes ran and stood in the sunlight.

"This is it!" she cried. "This is where we're gonna see it! Unicorns, here we come."

Agnes emptied her backpack on the ground, making a pile of marshmallows, licorice, lollipops, and chocolate.

"What's that for?" Edith asked.

"Bait!" Agnes grabbed Edith's hand and dragged her behind a large rock. "Now all we have to do is wait."

Hours later, Edith and Agnes were still hiding behind the rock. Every time Edith had tried to get up, Agnes had insisted they stay just a little longer. She was certain a unicorn would come eventually.

Edith yawned. She loved Agnes, but how long were they supposed to wait?

"Can we go back now?" Edith asked finally.

"Already?" Agnes said. "Just a couple more hours!"

"We have to be home before it gets dark," Edith tried. "Plus, you know, I put itching powder in Fritz's underwear drawer, and I don't want to miss all the fun."

Agnes stared at the pile of bait in the middle of the clearing. It was right where they had left it. "I don't understand," she said, sighing. "I did exactly what the man said."

"Right," Edith said, trying to think of the right words to say. "You mean that one-eyed, scar-faced man that everybody laughed at? Look, Agnes, maybe we're not—"

Before she could finish her sentence there was a rustling in the bushes. Something was out there—something was coming for the bait. Agnes stared at a nearby bush. There was something behind it . . . something furry and white.

"My whole life has been building to this moment!" she whispered.

Just then a goat burst through the bush. It was small and white. And it was missing one horn.

"Um," Edith started. "It's a—"

"Unicorn!" Agnes cried. She ran and hugged the tiny goat. "I can't believe it! I'm gonna name you Lucky!"

The goat licked Agnes's nose. Edith opened

her mouth to explain how it wasn't a unicorn, how it was really just a goat with one horn, and that unicorns didn't really exist—but then she saw Agnes's face. She'd never seen Agnes so happy.

"Yeah," she said under her breath as Agnes hugged the unicorn's neck. "I'll let someone else burst her bubble. . . ."

CHAPTER 18

Dru's doorbell rang. When Lucy opened it, the little Freedonian boy from the cheese festival was standing outside. He held a piglet in his hands.

"Hello, mother of Margo," he said. "I am Niko. I present you with pig to confirm my engagement to your daughter."

Lucy let out a loud, raucous laugh, but then her expression turned serious. "Hey . . . what now?" she said.

Margo came up behind her, noticing Niko standing on the front steps.

He raised his eyebrow at her and smiled. "Hello, my schmoopsie poo," he cooed.

"Whoa! Hey!" Margo took a step back.

"He seems to think you're engaged," Lucy explained.

"What?" Margo was horrified. "We're not engaged!"

"But you took bite of engagement cheese!" Niko cried.

"But I didn't know it was engagement cheese!" Margo said. "And how is engagement cheese even a thing?"

She turned to Lucy, raising her eyebrows as if to say *Help me out here!* Lucy knew it was technically her fault. If she hadn't insisted Margo go onstage at the cheese festival, this never would've happened.

"Look, Niko," Lucy tried. "You seem like a very nice boy. With a very nice pig. But you are not engaged. Okay? It's not happening."

Niko's shoulders slumped. "I understand. Who was I kidding? A dumpling like me with a goddess like you? But I promise: I will never forget you, Margo. Never."

He turned, leaving with the pig.

"Oh, I'm pretty sure I won't forget you, either," Margo said as the door slammed behind him.

Lucy let out a deep breath.

"Wow, that was crazy!" she said. "*Wooo!*"

"*That* was totally humiliating!" Margo snapped. "Taking a bite of that cheese was the stupidest thing I've ever done. Why did I listen to you?"

"Right, but it's over now, so—"

Knock knock knock!

Lucy turned back to the door. How many times did she have to tell this kid? No engagement. Ever. Never gonna happen.

But when she opened the door, Niko was standing next to a round, angry-looking woman carrying a baby. "You!" the woman yelled. "You refuse my son's engagement pig? May you and your daughter die a slow death and be buried with onions!"

She spat. The baby spat.

"Alright, lady," Lucy said, having had enough. "That's it! Okay, I know we are visitors here, and yes, your country has some pretty messed-up traditions, but nobody—*nobody!*—curses my daughter! You got that?"

Lucy poked her finger into the woman's chest, backing her down off the porch.

"Because if you mess with Margo," she said, yelling now, "you mess with me! And I promise, you do not want to mess with me! *Do you understand?*"

"Yes, yes," Niko's mother said, running away.

Lucy turned back to Margo, not sure what to say. This was all her fault. Margo had every right to be furious, and if she didn't speak to her for ages, she would just have to deal with—

Margo threw her arms around Lucy, hugging her tight. Lucy was startled at first, but then she wrapped her arms around her daughter, pulling her close. She'd been waiting for this moment for so long. To finally feel like Margo loved her as much as she loved Margo. To finally feel like a mom.

Just when Lucy was thinking she could stay like that forever, Margo pulled away. She ran off to her room without saying another word.

Lucy stood on the porch, stunned.

"I'm a mom," she said out loud. Then she smiled. "I've got to tell Gru!"

She turned to go back in the house when

she heard the sound of an engine firing up. She looked down at the water, noticing Gru and Dru in Dru's boat. They sped off over the water.

What were they doing? Why hadn't Gru told her they were going somewhere? And why on earth were they wearing spandex?

"Fritz!" she called, wandering through the house, looking for the butler. "Oh, Fritz!"

CHAPTER 19

The boat sped over the water. Gru was steering it, the wind in his face as they got closer to Bratt's lair.

"Look at us!" Dru called out. "Two brothers pulling a heist. And that diamond will make us the richest, most powerful villains in the world! Right, Brother?"

"Sure . . . ," Gru replied half-heartedly. He thought of his real plan of returning the diamond to AVL. He could still picture Valerie's smug face.

"Look, we're here!" Gru said, changing the subject. He pointed at the tower out in the middle of the water. Jagged, razor-sharp spikes jutted out all around the base of the fortress. "I'm going in. Take the wheel."

"I still don't see why I can't go with you," Dru said.

"Hey, we discussed this," Gru tried. "Now is not the time to mess with the plan."

Gru hit a button on the dashboard and *BOING!* He ejected himself from the boat and went flying toward the tower. Using the controls on his wrist, he cycled through different modes, eventually choosing STICKY. By the time he hit the building, he was as sticky as glue. His suit would now hold him in place as he climbed the tower.

He reached up, beginning his climb, when Dru crash-landed beside him. Dru hit the building hard, his face smashed flat. "Hey, Brother," he mumbled.

"What are you doing?" Gru cried. "I told you, you were supposed to stay in the boat!"

"I didn't think you meant that literally!" Dru said.

"What other way would I have meant it?" Gru asked. He let out a deep breath, knowing it was too late now. Dru was here, and he'd have to deal with it. "Alright. Let's move. Just follow my lead."

Dru lifted up one hand then immediately went tumbling down toward the spikes.

"Help me!" he yelled. "Ow, ow, oh no! The poison spikes! Oh, I'm gonna be impaled!"

Dru kept falling toward the bottom of the building, trying desperately to get his sticky suit to work. Finally, he stopped just inches from one of the spikes.

"Ha!" he called up, realizing he was still alive. "I'm okay!"

"Come on," Gru said, scaling the side of the building.

Dru hurried to catch up. But the security bot had already sensed something was off. Its red light was beeping as it swooped down to see Dru.

"It's a scanning device!" Gru hissed. "Quick—camouflage mode."

Dru hit the button on his wrist, cycling through all the different modes. Scuba, nope. Armor, nope. Flame, nope. He finally got to camouflage just as the bot flew by.

"Freeze!" Gru called down. "And close your eyes. And your mouth. Don't forget the mouth!"

Dru did what he was told. He tried to stay completely still as the bot scanned the side of the building, trying to detect if anyone was there. Gru watched, waiting to see what would happen, afraid this was it. Would it all end here? Would they be caught before they even got inside?

He held his breath, and then the security bot finally flew away. He began another long circle around the tower. Gru knew this was their chance.

"Take my hand!" he called down.

They climbed together toward a narrow ledge halfway up the tower. They were still a few yards from the top. Gru hit a button on his palm, filling the suit with an air bubble that looked (and felt) a lot like a fart. He floated up and up, his suit like a helium balloon.

"Follow me!" he called to Dru, who hit his own button.

Gru used sticky mode to stick to the side. He was right at the entrance to the lair—a small vent in the top, which was just big enough to climb in. He was about to enter when Dru flew toward him, totally out of control. He looked like a balloon that someone had untied—all the air was rushing out of his suit, making him do big, crazy loops in the air.

"Look out!" he yelled as he slammed into Gru.

The two brothers went tumbling through the vent and into the lair below.

CHAPTER 20

They bumped and bounced along the inside of the air shaft, plummeting toward the bottom. *SMASH!* They hit it hard, all the breath leaving their bodies. They lay there, feeling bruised and beaten.

"We got in!" Dru said after a beat.

Gru checked the screen on his wrist. It was a radar to help him locate the diamond. "Come on," he grumbled. "This way."

Gru crawled as fast as he could toward the diamond.

"Okay, finally!" he said. "It looks like it's right above us."

"Okay!" Dru said. "What do I do? Should I wait in the vent?"

"No," responded Gru. "Come with me."

Gru climbed up out of the vent. It looked like they were in Bratt's bedroom. He turned his back on Dru for a second and suddenly realized that Dru had sat down . . . at the foot of Bratt's bed. The villain wore a sleep mask as he snored away, clutching the diamond in both hands.

"Yes, I'd like to thank the Academy," Bratt murmured. "Yes, yes, Molly Ringwald. I will take you to prom."

Gru grabbed Dru, pulling him away from the bed. Then Gru reached out for the diamond. Dru pushed his brother aside, trying to reach the diamond as well. Then they started to struggle.

"There we—no, no!" mumbled Gru as he fought off his brother's grasp.

"I can do it—" insisted Dru.

"No, no, no, no, no! Don't, don't, don't!" Gru scolded him.

They went back and forth until Dru stepped on a toy on the floor, which made a loud beeping sound. Bratt's alarm went off.

"Who . . . Who's there . . . ?" Bratt grabbed for his sleep mask, pulling it off.

Dru and Gru rolled under the bed. They held their breath, hoping Bratt wouldn't notice them there. He didn't. But now he was up, wide awake, and walking around the lair. He grabbed the diamond and padded off.

When they were certain he'd left the room, Gru and Dru got up and started down the hallway. It was lined with rows and rows of vintage Balthazar Bratt action figures. They were the same ones from the eighties, with purple jumpsuits and eyes that lit up red.

"Dolls?" Gru asked, realizing they must've been the same action figures from Bratt's show. "Looks like Bratt was the only one stupid enough to buy this junk."

"Oh man!" Dru said, picking one up. "I used to have one of these! *Pew pew pew! Aaah! Oww!*"

Dru accidentally activated the doll's laser beam. Blinded, he dropped the doll to the ground.

"Hey! *Shh!* Come on!" said Gru. He kept going, gesturing for Dru to follow him into Bratt's lab. But as they walked out of the room, the doll's eyes started to glow red.

■ ■■ ■ ■■ ■ ● ⊖ ● ■ ■■ ■ ■■ ■

Inside the lab, there was a giant vat of bubbling pink gum.

"Gum!" Dru said, popping a piece in his mouth.

"Hey! Focus!" Gru snapped. "We're after the diamond, not the bubble gum!"

They approached another door and heard voices. Gru slid behind a crate with Dru close behind him. They both peered inside.

Bratt and his robot Clive were staring up at a giant Balthazar Bratt action figure. It was one hundred feet tall, with glowing red eyes. A ladder was resting against its head.

"And now to put this where it belongs," Bratt said, holding up the Dupont Diamond.

Gru leaned closer, trying to get a better look, but Dru was making gagging noises behind him. "Will you please shut up?" Gru asked. "He's gonna spot us."

When he turned back, Dru was twisting and turning, obviously in pain. The bubble gum was the same type that Bratt had used on the tanker ship. It expanded in Dru's mouth and was now coming out his nose. Gru tried to pull it out, but his hand stuck right to it.

"Spit it out!" Gru hissed. "Spit it out! I told you not to touch anything!"

Gru turned around, getting behind Dru to perform the Heimlich on him. That's all it took for Clive to sense them there.

"Intruders!" the robot yelled. "Intruders!"

Bratt ran into the lab, aiming his Keytar right at them.

"Gru!" he sneered. Then he turned to Dru. "There's two of you now? Then this will be twice as much fun."

Gru clutched his fist around Dru's belly, pushing down hard to clear the gum that was stuck in his throat. The gum flew out of Dru's mouth and hit Bratt and Clive, sticking them to the wall. Gru ran across the room, grabbed the diamond, and headed for the door.

"*Aaaaah!*" Bratt yelled, trying to break free of the gum. "Give me back my diamond! Total lockdown!! Go get 'em, Bratt Pack!!"

Alarms screeched. Lights flashed. One by one, each of the *Evil Bratt* action figures came alive and climbed down from the wall, their eyes glowing red. They took off after Gru and Dru.

"They're gonna get us!" Dru screeched. He was too afraid to move. "They're gonna get us!"

"Run!" Gru yelled. They started down the corridor, the action figures close behind them. Gru spotted a door ahead and leapt through the air, crashing into it. It shattered, and Gru and Dru ran through, ending up on the ledge outside.

All the lair's weapons were now armed. Missile launchers emerged from the sides of the building. More spikes shot up out of the water. The alarms continued blaring as Gru peered down the side of the tower, realizing they were stuck. There was no way they could get off the ledge now, and the army of Evil Bratts was coming for them.

"Oh no . . . ," Gru said, realizing how bad it was.

"*Oh no?*" Dru asked, panicked. "What does that mean? *ARE WE GONNA DIE?? ARE WE GONNA DIE?? WE'RE GONNA DIE!!*"

Gru looked around. For once, Dru was right. They were completely trapped. There was no way out. Gru had been in hundreds of terrible situations before, but none of them had been this bad.

A strange sound mixed with the blaring siren. Somewhere in the distance, Gru heard the *wup wup wup* of a helicopter. He turned, spotting Dru's red copter coming toward them, just low enough that they could climb on.

He glanced back inside. The Evil Bratts were so close, their weapons aimed at Gru and Dru as the army marched down the hall. The brothers were out of time.

"Dru! Gru!" Lucy yelled from the cockpit. She swooped down, getting as close to the tower as she could. "Hold on!"

Gru and Dru leapt into the helicopter and Lucy steered it out over the ocean, dodging missiles as they flew away from Bratt's lair. No one spoke until they were sure they were safe, with the giant purple tower disappearing behind them.

"Thank you for saving us!" Dru said,

staring at the dazzling diamond. "Look! We got the diamond! And we're going to—"

"Take it to the AVL to get our jobs back!" Gru said.

"Wait, *whaaa*?" Dru said, stunned. They were supposed to be in this together—brothers turned super villains. Just two buds bent on taking over the world.

"That's amazing!" Lucy said. "And the best part is you are never going to do anything behind my back ever again! Right?"

"Yup! Yup! Right," Gru said. "Lesson learned."

Gru glanced down at the diamond in his hands, feeling better than he had since that day at AVL. Maybe he'd made some mistakes, maybe he hadn't always been perfect, but he'd defeated Balthazar Bratt. And even though returning the diamond disappointed his brother, Gru had done something AVL couldn't—he'd gotten the Dupont Diamond back. He'd won.

He smiled, looking out over the ocean.

I won, he repeated to himself.